RECEIVED

1 4 NOV 2014

KT-559-607

30131 05323105 3

LONDON BOROUGH OF BARNET

PAUL MEETS BERNADETTE

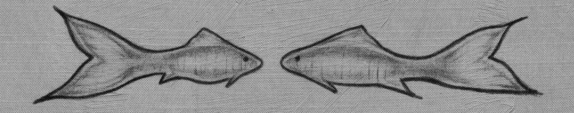

ROSY LAMB

WALKER BOOKS
AND SUBSIDIARIES
LONDON • BOSTON • SYDNEY • AUCKLAND

Paul used to go round in circles.

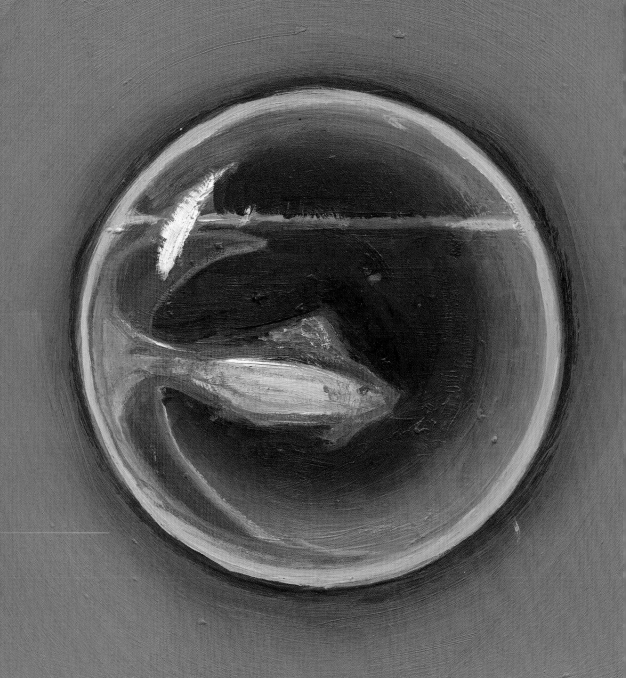

He made big circles

and little circles.

He circled from left to right

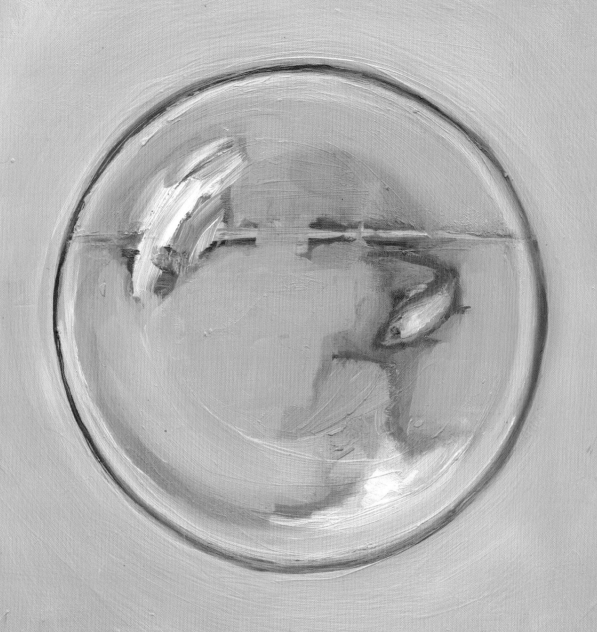

and from right to left.

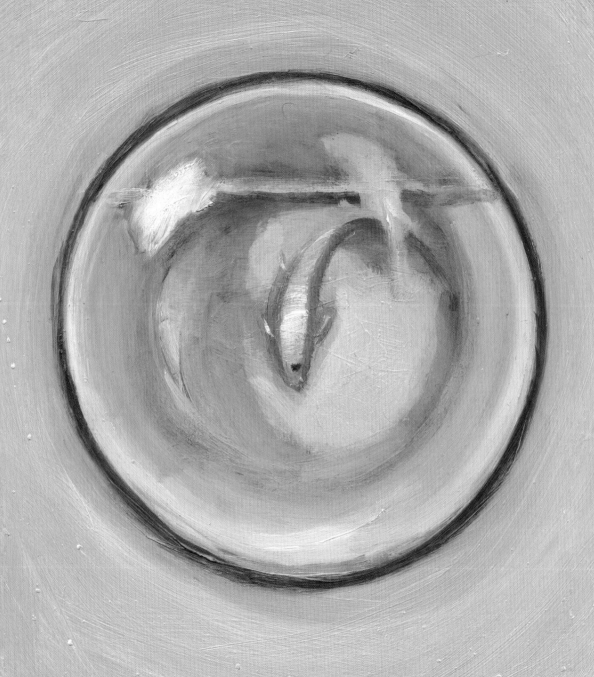

He circled from top to bottom

and from bottom to top.

And then one day, Bernadette dropped in.

"What are you doing?" Bernadette asks Paul.

"I'm going round and round," says Paul. "What else is there to do?"

"Haven't you ever noticed that there's a whole world out there? There are so many things to see. Come and look over here."

"What do you think that yellow thing is?"
asks Bernadette.

"Hum de dum..." says Paul.

"That," says Bernadette, "is a boat!"

"Paul, come over here," says Bernadette.

"Do you see the forest with trees of every colour?"

"Yes, I do," says Paul. "How enchanting!'

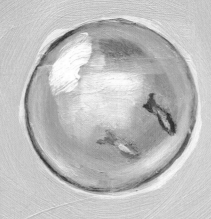

"Do you see that round thing off in the distance?
What do you think that is?" asks Bernadette.

"I just can't think," answers Paul.

"That," says Bernadette, "is a cactus!"

"Aha," says Paul. "And what is that draped up there?"

"Why, that is a lady's dress!"

"Oh, that is a dress! Of course, of course. What else could it be?" Paul says. "And I think it would look very pretty on you."

Paul spots something big and blue. "What is that?"
he asks Bernadette.

"That," says Bernadette, "is an elephant."

"Is she a dangerous elephant?" asks Paul.

"She is not *too* dangerous," Bernadette tells Paul. "But you must not disturb her when she is feeding her babies."

"Look up, over there!" Bernadette exclaims.

"A lunetta butterfly!"

How lovely she is, thinks Paul.

"And do you see the tall buildings over there?" says Bernadette. "That is a city."

"What is the name of the city?" asks Paul.

"Milkton Keynes," Bernadette tells him.

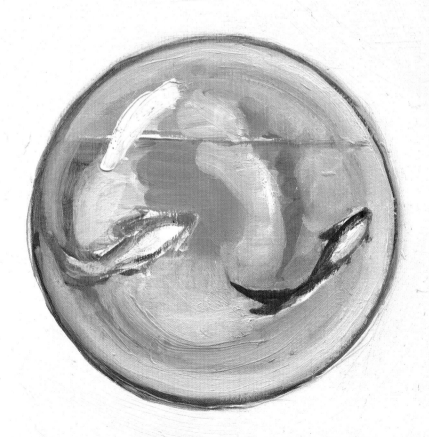

"Are those two bright-yellow circles down there fried eggs?" Paul asks Bernadette.

"Are you crazy?" says Bernadette. "Of course they are not fried eggs! That is the sun and the moon!"

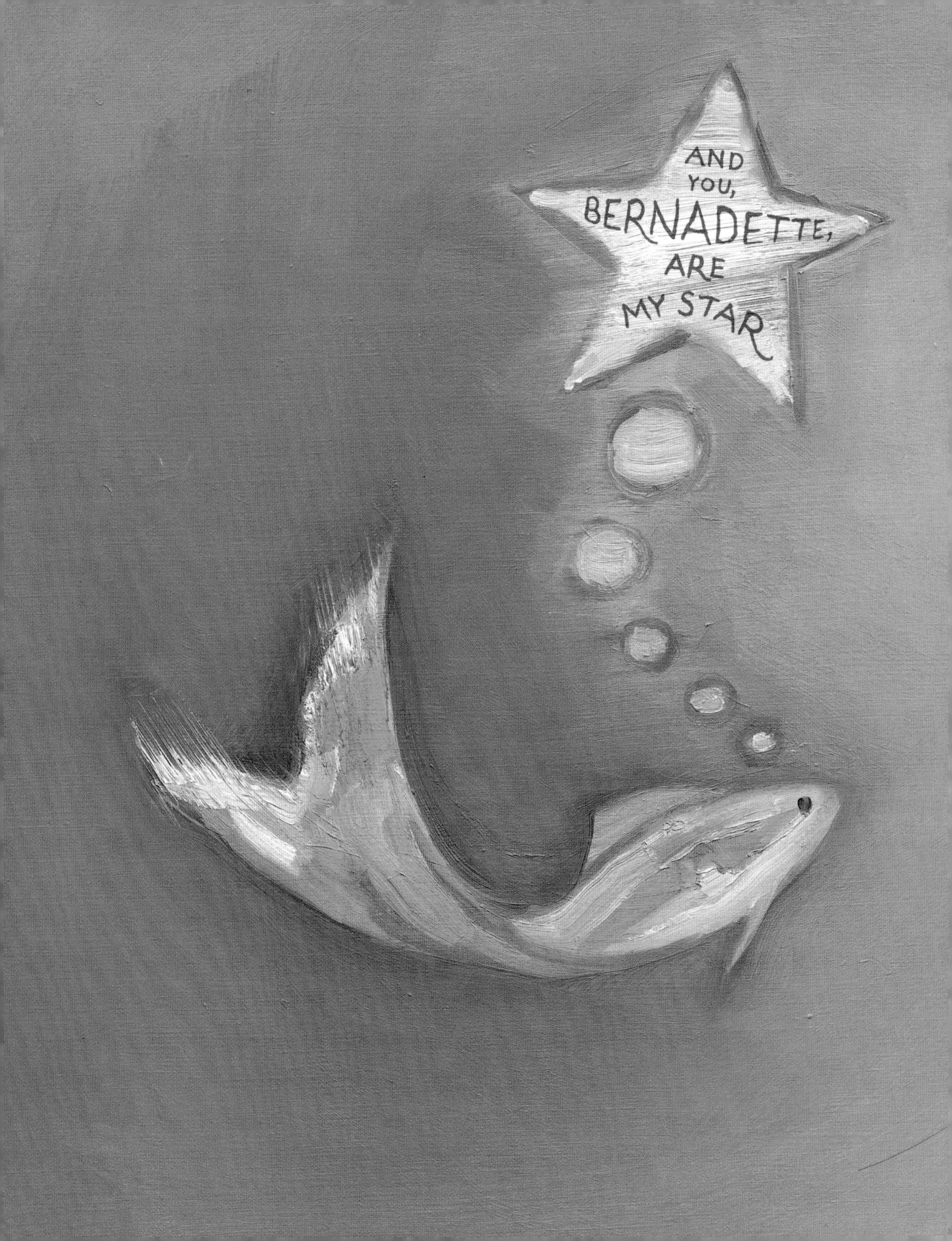
AND YOU, BERNADETTE, ARE MY STAR

"There is just one more thing in
the whole world," says Bernadette.
"What is it?" asks Paul.
Bernadette motions down below
and tells him, "It's a ...

fish!"

Bernadette has shown Paul the whole world,
and so Paul doesn't go round in circles any more.
He has something so much better to do.

Now Paul goes round Bernadette.

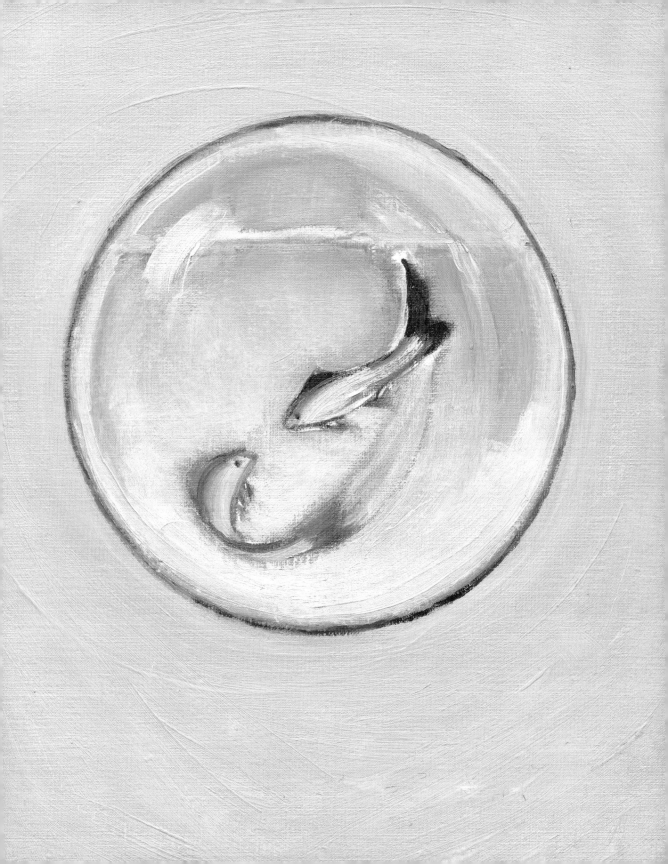

For Meena, my little fish

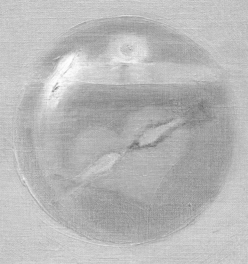

Thanks to the art director, Maryellen Hanley, whose clarity of
vision shows at every turn of the page, and to my husband, Karthik,
for helping me dust off the little book I mocked up years ago.

First published 2014 by Walker Books Ltd
87 Vauxhall Walk, London SE11 5HJ

2 4 6 8 10 9 7 5 3 1

© 2013 Rosy Lamb

The right of Rosy Lamb to be identified as author/illustrator of this work has been
asserted by her in accordance with the Copyright, Designs and Patents Act 1988

This book has been typeset in Hightower

Printed in China

All rights reserved. No part of this book may be reproduced, transmitted or
stored in an information retrieval system in any form or by any means,
graphic, electronic or mechanical, including photocopying, taping and
recording, without prior written permission from the publisher.

British Library Cataloguing in Publication Data:
a catalogue record for this book is available from the British Library

ISBN 978-1-4063-4792-0

www.walker.co.uk